Drawings to Live With

End papers from a drawing by Raoul Dufy

BRYAN HOLME

Vertes

Also by Bryan Holme: PICTURES TO LIVE WITH

Drawings to Live With

THE VIKING PRESS   NEW YORK

To Julian Christopher

The author wishes to express his sincere thanks to the artists whose drawings appear on these pages, and to acknowledge his gratitude to the collectors, museums, art galleries, and publishers who have also graciously given permission for the reproduction of their treasures. These names appear at the end of each description. Inevitably some of the originals will have changed hands since the photographs were first made available; in these cases and the few instances where the proprietor is unknown, the author also wishes to make due acknowledgment. His heartfelt thanks go to Elfrida Holme for her constant assistance, to Annis Duff and Velma Varner for their most valuable guidance, and to the wonderful team at The Viking Press who have worked so valiantly in the editing, production, and launching of this book.

Contents

No Two Alike

Everything under the sun has been drawn a million and one times, yet no two interpretations are exactly alike. Each tree, flower, and animal of its own kind differs, and every human being too has an individual twist to his character which in turn influences the way he sees and draws the world about him. Even when an artist wishes to copy a drawing, or make a tracing of it, some slight divergence always occurs in the direction or weight of a line. It is impossible for a human being to do precisely the same thing twice, and this is one of the reasons why the subject of drawing—as of life itself—can be endlessly fascinating.

The urge to create something beautiful is a very basic one, and should this lead a person to express himself graphically, rather than through words or music, he might equally well take up drawing, painting, or sculpture, or try his skill in one of a hundred other ways as different as designing a house, a garden, or a model boat. But it is an interesting fact that nearly all these other activities require a plan, and therefore a drawing, before they can take shape. If you wanted a house built in a certain way, you can imagine the kind of thing that might happen if you told the builder to go ahead without giving him some kind of a drawing or blueprint to follow. The result could resemble anything from an igloo to a half-baked version of the Taj Mahal.

Some drawings—and good ones, too—evolve from those spontaneous little scribbles worried out while you are trying to think of what next to say in a letter, or that are made during a long talk on the telephone which somehow seems to require that the hand be kept as busy as the conversation. The mere sight of a clean piece of paper is

Prehistoric man also had the urge to draw, as can be seen from these giraffe, boldly outlined on a rock in Africa thousands of years ago. (Rock engravings in Habeter, Fezzan. Photo: Frobinius Institute.)

Blackboard drawing by a child of eight.

temptation enough for some people to find a pencil to scribble with, and is there a living soul who has gazed at a large, empty blackboard without feeling the urge to make the most glorious drawing all over it in chalk?

Many graduate from blackboard drawing and become skilled enough to make art their career. This can still call for a sketch composed of relatively few lines, as displayed in the pen drawing opposite, or it might involve an enormously detailed composition such as the one shown on the next two pages. Although some drawings may be even simpler than El Greco's head, and some more elaborate than Brueghel's "Alchemist's Shop," together these two provide a fascinating study in contrasts.

When we consider that drawings are made for so very many purposes—to be exhibited as works of art in a gallery or a museum, to illustrate books, magazines, or advertisements, to serve as outlines for painting or sculpture, as blueprints for architecture, or as designs for engines, automobiles, or one of a thousand other three-dimensional objects—we realize what an astonishing variety of line can be brought to life from the tip of a simple pencil or pen or brush.

Opposite: This sketch by El Greco and the drawing by Brueghel over the page demonstrate how simple or how enormously detailed a drawing can be. ("Head of a Woman." El Greco. Pïnakotek, Munich.)

Overleaf: The engraving on the next two pages shows a corner of an alchemist's shop in medieval Holland. And what a wild and wonderful combination of people, pots, pans, tools—and ideas—the frenzied scene presents. ("The Alchemist's Shop." Pieter Brueghel. Metropolitan Museum of Art.)

A man who drew for many purposes was Leonardo da Vinci, a genius of sixteenth-century Florence and one of the great men of all time. Leonardo drew for pleasure, as every artist must; he drew because he could not help drawing. He made sketches as preliminary studies for his "Mona Lisa" and for other oil paintings; and

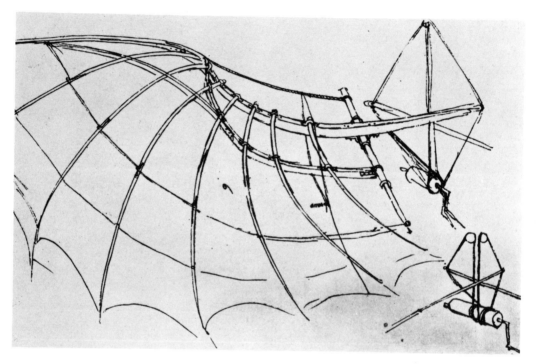

An experimental design for a flying machine. ("Wing with Crank Device." Leonardo da Vinci. From his Codex on the Flight of Birds.)

he also dreamed of many things which, after he had committed them to paper, turned out to be momentous inventions. These varied from revolutionary agricultural instruments and war weapons, built in his own day, to a prototype of the flying machine, which man kept trying to perfect until in our own century he succeeded.

Some of Leonardo's drawings are mere outlines of ideas, as is the one above; others were conceived as works of art, as was the magnificently drawn head of a warrior on the facing page.

Opposite: Leonardo drew this profile in 1475, and it is suggested that he himself was the model. ("Warrior in Ceremonial Helmet." Leonardo da Vinci. British Museum.)

Although art is a serious business, not all art is serious in content. As in life itself, there is light as well as shadow, gaiety, wit, and humor as well as sorrow, and tinsel mixed with solid gold. In one way or another, every aspect of life is reflected in the drawings that follow, according to the way the artist has seen it.

Leonardo wrote, "If the painter wishes to see the enchanting beauties, he has the power to produce them. If he wishes to see monstrosities, whether terrifying, ludicrous, laughable or pitiful, he has the power and authority to create them. If he wants valleys, if from high mountain tops he wants to survey vast stretches of country, if beyond he wants to see the horizon or the sea, he has power to create all this . . . indeed whatever exists in the universe, whether in essence, in art, or in the imagination, the painter has first in his mind and then in his hands." So it was that man first set about to draw and has, ever since, created pictures for us to enjoy and to live with.

Sketch by Leonardo.   (British Museum.)

Three Ways of Drawing

The closer the subject of a drawing is to nature itself, the harder it is to tell in which century the work originated. In other words, a man has always been a man, flowers have always been flowers, and cats have always been cats. But as soon as the artist draws a man fully dressed, or places flowers on a table in a room, or draws a cat in a street, the kind of dress or furniture or street architecture—whichever the case may be—will usually have changed sufficiently with the times to make the period of the drawing quite easy to identify. Today, for instance, if an artist were accurately to represent a street scene in Florence, instead of drawing the princely Medicis, or carriages, carts, and horses, he would (unless he was imagining how the city used to look) draw people in modern dress window shopping, eating at outdoor cafés, or roaring up the street in Fiats and Ferraris. Only some of the buildings would look the way they did in sixteenth-century Florence. Furthermore, the design of cars changes every year, and this dates a picture perhaps even faster than fashions in clothes.

But apart from the period and subject matter of a drawing, and allowing for the individual character of the artist, which shows through in any work he does (some artists are bold, some are gentle, some are neat, and others are dreadfully untidy), there are only a few basic ways in which any artist *can* draw what he sees.

At the risk of oversimplification, it might be said that there are three broad classifications of style. One of these, the so-called classic, or academic, style, is seen in the portrait on the next page.

This classic pen and water-color portrait of a young princess, whose eyes follow us no matter from what angle we look at her, is one of the greatest drawings that the sixteenth century produced. ("Elizabeth of Saxony." Lucas Cranach the Younger. Kupferstichkabinett, Berlin.)

Opposite: Here the artist attempted to draw everything exactly as his eye saw it. The head, dignified and erect, is perfectly proportioned, and in the flowing beard hardly a hair would appear to have been missed. ("Head of a Bearded Man." Francesco Salviati. Pierpont Morgan Library.)

1502

Dürer's approach was equally realistic. Drawings of this kind—and paintings too—in which every little detail is included, are usually referred to as "representational." To our eyes today, they appear almost photographic in their completeness. Dürer lived in the sixteenth century, but the same kind of clear, painstaking work has been produced by artists in every century since, including our own, as we see on page 21.

Opposite: Another example of how detailed and realistic a drawing can be. You can see the creature breathing—almost. ("Hare." Albrecht Dürer. Albertina Museum, Vienna.)

No one has ever drawn hands better than Dürer, and he made several studies of them like these, held quietly in prayer. ("Hands." Albrecht Dürer. Museum of Fine Arts, Budapest.)

Opposite: Modern or medieval? It could almost be either, but it is by a twentieth-century American artist working in the finest classic tradition. ("Sister of Charity." Robert Vickrey. Midtown Galleries.)

The clothes immediately tell us that this attractive family lived in the nineteenth century. But the technique of the drawing differs remarkably little from the work of earlier masters. ("Guillon-Lethière Family." J. A. D. Ingres. Museum of Fine Arts, Boston.)

The next three pages introduce a second, very different kind of drawing. While the artists Guardi, Goya, and Daumier have sketched their subjects in a natural and completely recognizable way, they have abandoned detail in an attempt to create more lively and dramatic effects. Through the use of animated, almost scribbly lines—as opposed to the studied lines of a formal, classic drawing—the essence or spirit of a scene has been stressed. To keep this kind of drawing flowing with movement, the artist works fast, allowing himself the liberty of many random strokes which have a way of adding warmth and animation to a picture. This type of work is referred to as "impressionistic" or "expressionistic" and it became the basis of a new way of painting in the late nineteenth century.

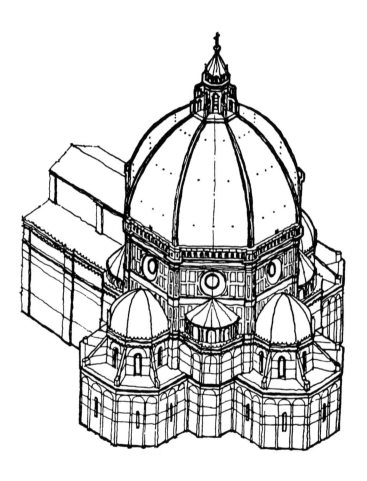

The illustration at left is introduced to show how an architect's very exact way of rendering a building contrasts with the way an artist—as opposite—makes a picture of one. ("The Duomo, Florence." After the design of Filippo Brunelleschi.)

Opposite: Here the feeling of light, air, and movement impresses us. Even the cathedral is alive with sunshine. Using a free, relaxed technique, the Venetian artist has kept the important details strong and clear, while using fainter lines to suggest others. It is the spirit of the scene that Guardi emphasizes, rather than the exact architectural features of the cathedral. ("Facade of St. Mark's." Francesco Guardi. Metropolitan Museum of Art.)

A grim drama in which our attention is immediately drawn to the thrust of the upper body as the man reaches over and stabs his victim. Detail has been sacrificed to strengthen the impression of force on the part of the aggressor, and of utter helplessness on the part of the dying man. ("The Stabbing." Francisco de Goya. Metropolitan Museum of Art.)

Opposite: In what resembles a triple exposure, several quick moments are combined in one as the entertainer, standing firmly on a chair, goes into his act to the accompaniment of a drum. ("A Clown." Honoré Daumier. Metropolitan Museum of Art.)

A stylish nineteenth-century scene, drawn at a time when artists in Paris had started to paint in an impressionistic manner—an approach long since suggested by a free, informal way of drawing. ("At the Opera." Constantin Guys. Private Collection.)

Opposite: Filled with life and character, this confident-looking clown stands in the ring with his pony and poodle. ("At the Circus." Henri de Toulouse-Lautrec. The Art Institute of Chicago.)   27

The movement of the horses and jockeys, and the tenseness of the spectators on the sideline are strongly conveyed by two opposing masses of bold strokes and scribbles. ("The Races." Édouard Manet. Museum of Fine Arts, Boston.)

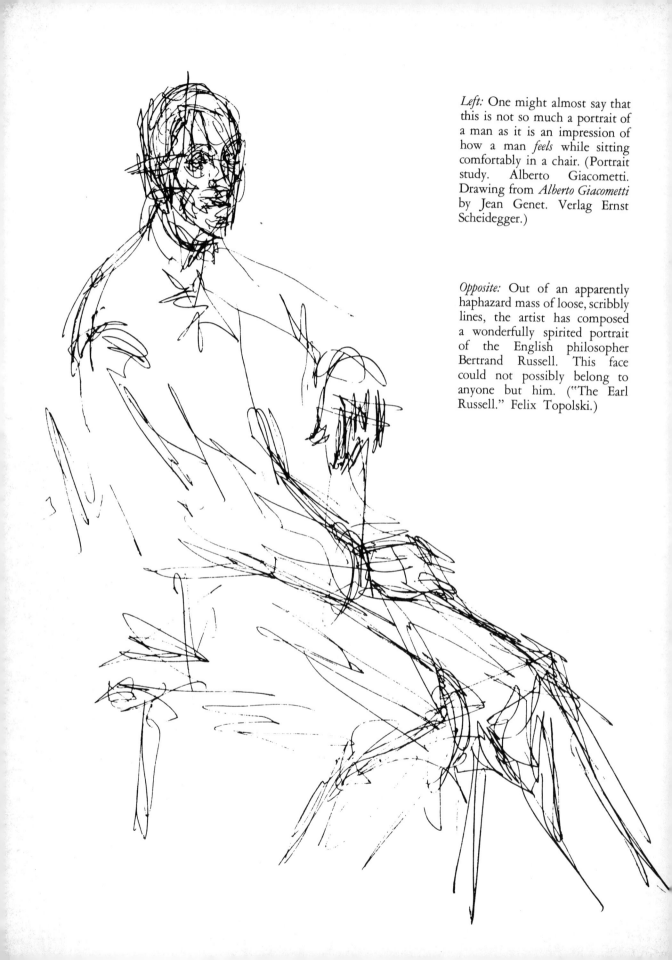

Left: One might almost say that this is not so much a portrait of a man as it is an impression of how a man *feels* while sitting comfortably in a chair. (Portrait study. Alberto Giacometti. Drawing from *Alberto Giacometti* by Jean Genet. Verlag Ernst Scheidegger.)

Opposite: Out of an apparently haphazard mass of loose, scribbly lines, the artist has composed a wonderfully spirited portrait of the English philosopher Bertrand Russell. This face could not possibly belong to anyone but him. ("The Earl Russell." Felix Topolski.)

32

This picture was more revolutionary when it was done in 1930 than it appears to our eyes today, yet the continuous, almost abstract meander of line that forms the man's head and joins one feature to another is original—and unendingly fascinating. ("The Mocker Mocked." Paul Klee. Museum of Modern Art.)

Opposite: An image that few people are likely to forget. And with what magic of line Topolski has brought to life not only the man but one of his most typical expressions. ("John F. Kennedy." Felix Topolski.)

33

Silhouettes rely entirely on outline for their effect. The lively trio above, copied exactly from a prehistoric painting, suggest how strongly artists today, many of them, are influenced by the work of the primitives. (Rock painting of three women walking. Valtorta Gorge, Spain. Drawing from *Die Felsbilder Europas* by Herbert Kühn.)

A simplification of the impressionistic type of work is to be seen in the pen drawing opposite. Here Picasso has used the fewest possible strokes to outline a girl's head, and what a sharp contrast there is between this modern "impression" and Cranach's portrait of the pretty Elizabeth of Saxony on page 17. Each drawing is, in its own way, superb. Drawings in outline are very difficult to bring off successfully. A head, without any shading or any lines other than the contour of the face, eyes, nose, and lips, could be very dull indeed, but in the expert hand of Picasso, how alive and interesting this portrait becomes through the use of slight but most telling distortions.

Opposite: In contrast with the portraits on the previous pages, a minimum of lines were used to make this simple and very clear statement. The technique may look easy, but enormous skill is required to draw this well. ("Head of a Girl." Pablo Picasso. Private collection.)

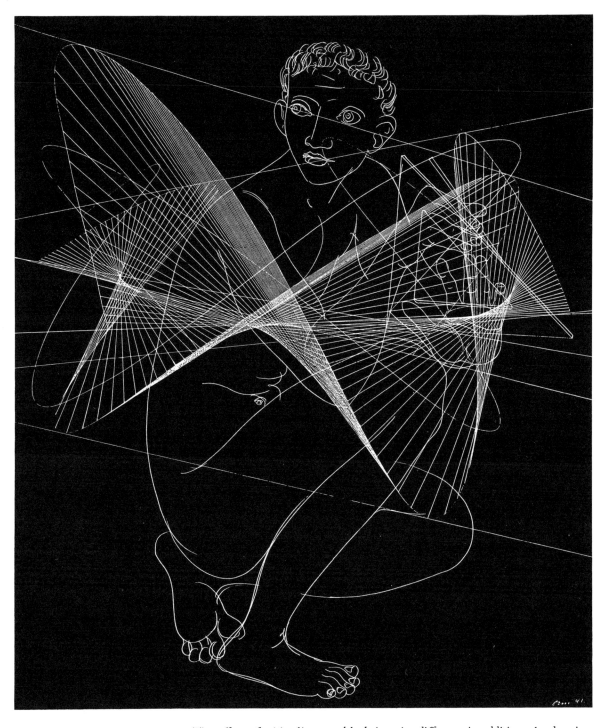

The effect of white lines on black is quite different; in addition, the drawing above is more controlled. The precise yet sweeping lines which flow from the man's hands are symbolic of his profession. He sees the world in terms of design. ("The Draughtsman." Hans Erni. Private collection.)

Opposite: Matisse also used slight and purposeful distortions to create a very alive impression of a woman in a Rumanian blouse. ("Portrait of a Lady." Henri Matisse. Fogg Museum of Art.)

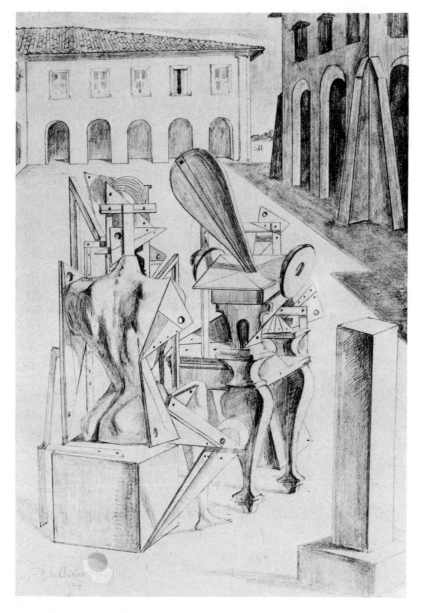

Left: This drawing of 1917 represents the start of the so-called "surrealist" movement, in which artists combined fantasy with a certain amount of fact. The two geometric figures, composed largely of the tools of their trade, sit facing each other enigmatically in a quite realistic setting. ("The Mathematicians." Giorgio de Chirico. Museum of Modern Art.)

Opposite: Two piercing eyes gaze out of a cagelike head. The perfect symmetry of the spiralling lines and the dramatic use of colored pencil on black paper make this semiabstract work extremely effective. ("Head." Pavel Tchelitchew. Museum of Modern Art.)

There is only one other basically different type of drawing, and this more closely parallels its equivalent in painting: the geometric, or abstract, picture. Artists who follow this modern trend are concerned mainly with how to arrange lines and solid forms in harmonious and well-balanced black-and-white patterns. In paintings, texture and color also play a very important part. In abstract art nothing is represented as the eye actually sees it in nature. Yet through the clever arrangement of lines, forms, and areas of light and dark, pleasing and sometimes very exciting compositions can be made.

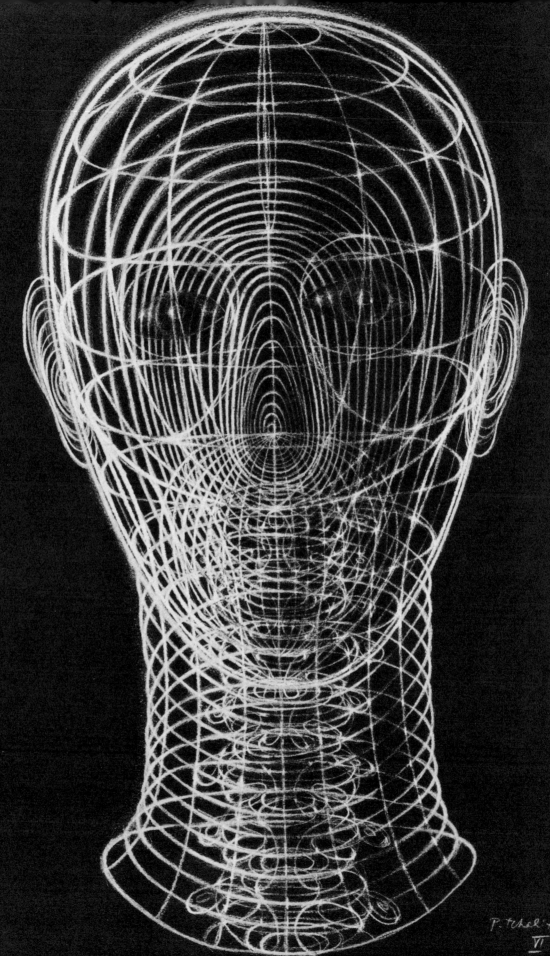

P. Tchelitchew
VI 1950

Provided that the general appearance of an abstract design appeals to us at the outset, interpreting it in our own particular way can be interesting and fun. The one below, for instance, is likely to suggest different things to different people.

In a sense, the liking for abstract art is an acquired taste. Yet when we walk through the streets of a modern city and look up at groups of tall buildings with glass facades, we see in reflection all kinds of abstract images composed of angles, contours, and reflected lines, as well as combinations of color that constantly change as day passes into night. Perhaps much of abstract drawing is, in fact, suggested by our modern cityscapes. And, usually, the simpler the lines used, the more dramatic is the total effect.

The appeal of this and other abstract drawings lies largely in well-organized forms and areas of pattern. (Composition. Wassily Kandinsky.)

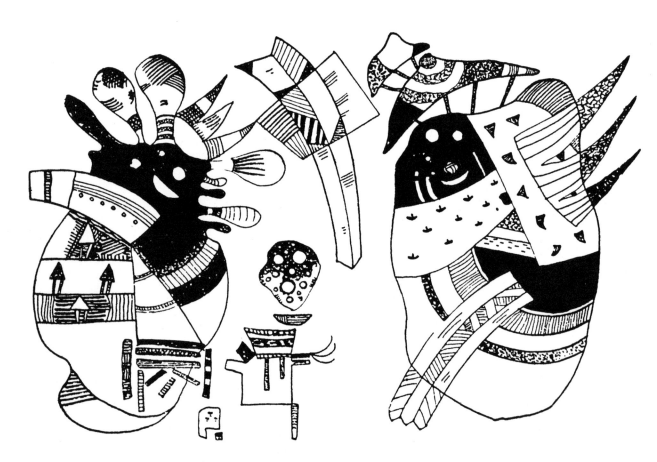

Like a note of music, no simpler statement could be made. Very important to the balance of the composition is the small white dot within the vertical line. Place a finger over it, and you will see how much the design loses. (Untitled drawing. Alexander Liberman. Betty Parsons Gallery.)

Sketches

Some of the most spirited drawings of all are to be found in sketchbooks. These are the quick studies from life that artists make for themselves, usually without thought that they will ever be bought by a museum or a collector.

The speed with which an artist should always be prepared to work is suggested in the remark that the painter Delacroix made to Baudelaire: "A man throws himself out of the fourth-floor window: if you can't make a sketch of him before he gets to the ground, you will never do anything big."

Wherever he goes, the artist is always looking at the world in terms of how interesting he can make some aspect of it appear on paper or canvas. The way a landscape composes itself, the expression of joy, sorrow, or excitement on someone's face, the beauty of a flower or the grace of a figure, the quick movement of a cat or of two dogs brawling in the street—whatever he sees that interests him he notes down and keeps for future reference.

As the point of view of each artist is different, so too is his skill with a pencil. Consequently we often see uninteresting drawings of beautiful subjects and interesting drawings of quite ugly ones. Fortunately we also see beautiful things beautifully drawn, and this is the kind of work that usually best stands the test of time.

Frequently the sketches an artist makes directly from life are better than the careful drawings or paintings he develops from his notes later on in the studio. Most professionals admit that it is very hard to recapture the spontaneity of a first impression, and almost impossible to repeat the speedy, expressive pencil strokes made during the first encounter with the subject.

One of the most justly famous drawings in the world is the main figure opposite, which Michelangelo sketched for a detail in the ceiling he was painting at the Sistine Chapel in Rome. (Sketches for the Libyan Sibyl. Michelangelo. Metropolitan Museum of Art.)

In Renaissance times most paintings were commissioned by the Church, and this usually entailed a preliminary sketch which the artist had to submit for his sponsor's approval. The drawing might be as complete and superbly executed as the one reproduced above. ("Annunciation." Jacopo Bellini. Louvre.)

Raphael made this sketch as a detail for a painting. Although he died at the age of thirty-seven, Raphael was one of the most prolific artists of all time. Often he made drawings for his paintings and, except for the final touches, left most of the work for his pupils to do in the studio. (Study for "The Descent from the Cross." Raphael. Metropolitan Museum of Art.)

Sometimes artists sketch from life at random, merely for the prac-
tice, and sometimes they go out to search for a particular model.
Few today would choose these fierce creatures (if indeed they could
find them), but in Cranach's day boar hunts were common and
therefore a typical subject to draw and paint. ("Wild Boars and
Dogs." Lucas Cranach the Elder. Kupferstichkabinett, Berlin.)

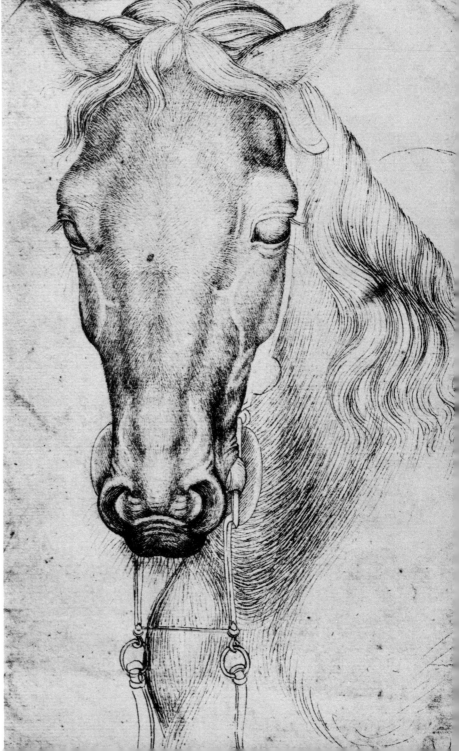

In the eighteenth century, Venice was the liveliest, gayest city in
the world. And here, in a sketch filled with mood, elegance, and the

atmosphere of the era, is an intimate glimpse of a candlelit masquerade.
("The Masked Ball." Francesco Guardi. Art Institute of Chicago.)

Géricault

The nineteenth-century French artist Géricault had two great passions—horses and painting. The "Frightened Horse" (opposite), in the Detroit Institute of Art, and the study above demonstrate how sketches made directly from life are often the most spirited—and dateless—of all. (Studies of horses. Théodore Géricault.)

51

The artist made this satiric sketch with the hurried point of a pen—
and possibly, too, with his tongue in cheek. ("Two Lawyers."
Honoré Daumier. Victoria and Albert Museum. Crown copyright.)

The charming study below is contemporary, but it could just as well have been done yesterday as today—or tomorrow. (Study of a cat. Clare Newberry.)

A few sweeping and agitated lines cleverly sum up the essence of the subject. Not only are these dancers, but we see that they are, quite specifically, ballet dancers, drawn in classical poses but in a modern way. ("Ballet." Emlen Etting. Midtown Galleries.)

Pen, Pencil, and Chalk

To most people a drawing means a sketch made with a pencil, probably because this is the handiest tool for the purpose in the average household. But professional artists draw with pencils—the many kinds of them—only part of the time. More master drawings have in fact been done in crayon or chalk, as was the delicate study by Watteau on page 64, or in pen and ink (sometimes with the addition of a wash), which was Rembrandt's choice on page 61. Still other drawings are made with charcoal or pastel, examples of which are included on the pages that follow.

Wash drawings are produced in much the same way as a water color, but instead of employing all the hues of the rainbow, the artist selects one, or perhaps two, neutral tones to preserve or enhance the quality of his drawing. In the past even a full water color was essentially a pencil or pen drawing filled in with color, as on page 17, and in the hunting scene on page 62. When the drawn part of a water color plays a more important part than the painted areas it is correct to call it a drawing, but when the major part of the picture is in color with little or no visible line work, it is more correct to classify it as a painting. There are borderline cases, of course, such as "The Locomotive" by Dong Kingman (page 74), which qualifies equally as a drawing and as a painting. The same can be said of the pastel study on page 66.

Each tool produces a particular quality of line, and the effect varies further according to the texture and color of the paper used. What an artist chooses to work with—and on—depends on his subject and the effect he wishes to produce. An architectural drawing usually calls for distinct lines, perhaps best defined with a pencil or pen on a rather hard-surface paper. On the other hand, a portrait of a furry animal or a drawing of a misty day might look better in chalk or pastel, drawn, possibly, on a colored paper.

Degas made this copy of the head from da Vinci's famous painting "Madonna of the Rocks." He selected a soft-lead pencil for the purpose, and how delicately he handled this most familiar of drawing tools. ("Woman's Head." Edgar Degas. Museum of Modern Art.)

57

A typical scene in old Holland, drawn with pen and bistre, with touches of blue. Bistre, a brown-colored paste made from soot, was common in the sixteenth century, but today artists obtain the same kind of effect with brown ink. ("Village with Boats and a Pier." Attributed to Jan Brueghel. Pierpont Morgan Library.)

60   A half-length portrait in pen and ink by the great Spanish painter
of the seventeenth century. (Portrait sketch. Velázquez. Louvre.)

Rembrandt was a prolific draftsman as well as a great etcher and painter. Although in 1961 one of his canvases fetched the highest price hitherto paid for a work in oils, the artist died in poverty. The drawing below, done with pen and wash, is typical of his work in this medium. ("Esther and Mordecai." Rembrandt. Pierpont Morgan Library.)

Overleaf: Completely different in mood and theme is the wash drawing on the next page, executed by the last of the great Venetian masters. It was produced nearly a hundred years later than Rembrandt's work (above) yet, interestingly, it appears less modern. ("Punchinello, Dogs and Boar." Giovanni Battista Tiepolo. Fogg Museum of Art.)

Softness and great delicacy also distinguish this crayon drawing of a mother and child. The shaded areas were produced by gently rubbing the markings of the crayon. ("Gabrielle and Coco." Pierre Auguste Renoir. Perls Gallery.)

Opposite: The French artist Watteau used red, black, and white chalk for this charming portrait. The sensitive treatment of the alert face and the interesting triangular composition of the body contribute to its greatness as a drawing. ("Seated Woman." Antoine Watteau. Pierpont Morgan Library.)

No one has loved, drawn, and painted every aspect of the ballet more often or more beautifully than Degas. Among his best-known works is this magnificent study in pastel colors. Pastel is much like crayon and chalk, but being softer and more crumbly, it is that much harder to work with. ("Ballet Dancers Resting." Edgar Degas. Photo: Durand-Ruel, Paris.)

The drawing above and the one on the opposite page, both of which belong to the nineteenth century, show how different two portraits of the same period and drawn with the same material can be. ("Achille Empéraire." Paul Cezanne. M. M. A. Chappius, Paris.)

Opposite: The choice of conte crayon on a rough-surface paper helped Seurat to produce the strong grainy effect which is so characteristic of his work. ("Aman Jean." Georges Seurat. Metropolitan Museum of Art.)

The sad, haunted expression of the girl is accentuated by the dark hair and the shawl that slopes away from her shoulders. The artist used black crayon on a rough-textured surface. ("Head of a Girl." Vincent van Gogh. Museum of Modern Art.)

Years later van Gogh made this drawing with a reed pen. "To improve at anything," he wrote, "especially drawing, I think it's best to go on and on at it and never ease off." Here he suggested the sky with straight lines, the movement of the sea with stronger, wavy lines, and used bold, broken lines for the pounding surf in the foreground. ("Sailing Boats." Vincent van Gogh. National Gallery, Berlin.)

There are no definite rules about drawing, and very few rules, for that matter, about anything concerning the making of a work of art—for so much depends upon an artist's particular technique and also upon his mood and the tools he has available when he feels ready to work. Sometimes he finds it effective to use more than one implement in the same drawing, as we have seen. But whether he reaches for pen, pencil, chalk, or brush, it is always with the aim of making the best picture he possibly can. And should a drawing fail to be up to his usual standard, the wise artist scraps it and starts another one, having gained from the experience. This, both Chinese and Japanese artists particularly have done.

Opposite: The Chinese are masters at capturing the essence of plant life in simple expressive lines. In this branch of bamboo, each leaf was made with a quick stroke of the brush. ("Bamboo Study." Kuan Tao-shêng. Private collection.)

Below: Even in the most exotic aquarium, this handsome fish would be spectacular. The drawing was made for an eighteenth century natural history book, published in Germany. ("*Chartodon cornutus.*" Marcus Elieser Bloch.)

Overleaf: The locomotive on the next page is one of the last of a vanishing breed. After they have gone forever, such gay and lively water colors will continue to remind us what great personality the steam engine had. ("Locomotive." Dong Kingman. Private collection.)

The Universal Language

When we read a story, we are continuously called upon to visualize characters and places, and the more we are able to draw on our own experience, the sharper the images are likely to be.

Part of this stored-up experience is based upon pictures we have seen, and our memory of one or more of them can be particularly helpful when a story takes place in a distant land or century. Should a book transport us to sixteenth-century India, for instance, we could only try to imagine what the Prince's elephant looked like in all its colorful trappings unless we had already seen a drawing such as the one on the opposite page. Similarly our idea of a Chinese landscape or a street in Timbuktu would be far from accurate unless we had visited these places or had seen them illustrated.

The immediate advantage an illustration has over the written word is, of course, that everyone, no matter what language he speaks, understands it. Consequently the very same drawings, paintings, and photographs can be reproduced—and understood—in books, magazines, and newspapers issuing from Paris, London, New York, or any other city of the world. And the more this universal language of pictures informs us about how people of other cultures look, live, and create beautiful things, the more we can understand and feel at home with them.

The illustrations in this chapter show a few of the diverse ways artists of all countries and times have chosen to draw the same subjects. No matter how different each interpretation is from another, whatever the artist intended to convey about people, animals, flowers, or landscapes can be understood everywhere.

It is from illustrations of this kind that we learn much about the people, customs, and animals of other lands and centuries. Had we to *imagine* this scene in the India of three hundred years ago, we would certainly have missed many details, such as the jingling bells at the sides of the elephants. ("Fighting Elephants Viewed by Jahongir." Mughal. Metropolitan Museum of Art.)

Peonies are peonies in any language, but this Chinese interpretation has a special oriental quality of its own. ("Flowers." Unknown Chinese artist. British Museum.)

Opposite page: A drawing that is recognizably European, yet closer in style to the work of the Chinese than are most Western studies of flowers. ("Columbine." Albrecht Dürer. Albertina Museum, Vienna.)

Rabbits and hares have obviously remained unchanged since the day they leapt from the Ark. Audubon drew these specimens in the 1840s for his second mammoth portfolio, *The Viviparous Quadrupeds of North America.* ("Rabbits." John James Audubon. American Museum of Natural History.)

And this is how a hare looked in fifteenth-century
Verona. ("Study of a Hare." Pisanello. Louvre.)

Four pets sharing a meal, drawn with unmistakable affection by
an artist living in England. ("Young Rabbits." Vere Temple.)

Grace, alertness, softness—all are beautifully expressed in this late seventeenth-century portrait by a Persian. ("Deer." Unknown artist. Metropolitan Museum of Art.)

Left: Almost identical in expression and pose, yet so differently drawn, is the same creature seen through the eyes of a present-day artist in France. ("Deer." Henri Gaudier-Brzeska. Private collection.)

وازعجايب بزكوهى كه خوستر زا از جايكا مهاء بلند دراندازد قرب صديبنه وسيزوباينند اكاه بدود

What a surprise! The plummeting Persian goat appears much less concerned about his rapidly changing whereabouts than his rock-bound companion. Probably he was just showing off. ("Mountain Goat Falling." Manafi al-Hayawan. Pierpont Morgan Library.)

Opposite: When an artist adds poetic touches to a landscape, does it make the scene less real? To him, no—because, by drawing not only what he sees but what he *feels,* he is presenting an experience. This, in a sense, makes a picture more real. ("Mountains in Clouds." Kao K'o-Kung. Peking Palace Museum.)

A parallel to the thirteenth-century water color on the opposite page can be found in this painting of the Grand Tetons by a Chinese-American artist. Kingman's water color bears a marked resemblance to the work of his forefathers across the Pacific. He has done the same thing, but in a much younger way. ("Grand Tetons." Dong Kingman. Atlantic Art Association.)

Above: No language barrier interferes with what the Persian artist of four hundred years ago is saying to us today, or with what the young man on bended knee is saying to the lady of his affections. ("Love Scene." Ustad Muhammadè. Museum of Fine Arts, Boston.)

Opposite: Two centuries later and three thousand miles away, clothes have changed and so has the type of drawing. But boy meets girl and the situation is the same—almost. ("The Letter." Jean-Honoré Fragonard. The Art Institute of Chicago.)

What is it that makes a young animal so appealing? In a cub, this English artist finds it partly in his "woolly animation and twinkling beads for eyes." ("Baby Bear." Raymond Sheppard. From his *Drawing at the Zoo*. Studio.)

Opposite: You do not have to be a bear to appreciate the joy of climbing a tree, even if getting tangled in the branches is part of the act. How well the artist has used the curving lines of the tree to frame the cub, while balancing the picture with the spectators below. ("Three Bear Cubs." Unknown fifteenth-century Persian artist. Museum of Fine Arts, Boston.)

Right: According to the fable by Aesop, "acquaintance softens prejudices." Having nearly died with fear at his first chance encounter with the lion, the fox was less frightened the second time, and upon seeing the lion for the third time, boldly went up and commenced a familiar conversation. ("The Fox and the Lion." Unknown fourteenth-century French artist.)

It is interesting that the black lion is just as much a lion as the white one above. Although lions are neither black nor white, our eyes quickly adjust and interpret, as they do with a photograph in which color is represented in light-to-dark shades of gray. ("Lion." Charles Knowles. From his *Psalm Book*. Viking.)

Opposite: Obviously after a very satisfactory meal— fat, proud, happy, and serene. ("Big Sitting Cat." Joseph Glasco. Museum of Modern Art.)

The zodiac sign for people born between February 20 and March 20 is two fish. Above is one of a pair taken from an ancient manuscript. Although it is Persian, it looks rather like a Japanese design for a kite. ("Pisces" [Detail]. Unknown artist. From *The Book of Stars and Constellations*.)

A spoiled puss who wanted the best half of the fish—first. ("Hors d'Oeuvres." Peggy Bacon. Weyhe Gallery.)

Smiling, curious, sneering, hurt—four different expressions on an international circle of man's best friends. The drawing was made for a French story by a Hungarian-born artist who lived in New York. ("Dogs." Marcel Vertes.)

Monarch of all he surveys. A mandarin-like Peke with silky, curling hair and a plume of a tail, drawn by a Japanese artist who made his home in Paris. ("Pekinese." Tsugouhara Foujita. Weyhe Gallery.)

Prints

Museums and libraries often arrange exhibitions of drawings, but there is a big difference between attending an occasional show and having works of art to live with every day of the year. Not everyone can own an original drawing, but most people can afford a print.

A print can be a woodcut, an etching, a lithograph, or an engraving. It can also be an entirely mechanical reproduction such as those offered for sale at a museum desk, or that we see reproduced in books and magazines. But from a collector's point of view, a print is a picture that involves handwork and that is produced by any one of the four processes mentioned.

All prints require a preliminary drawing. The artist must then trace, copy, or otherwise transfer this drawing onto a block of wood, or a stone or metal surface, which can be carved or etched in such a way that the drawn lines stand out and the image will print clearly when the surface of the block is inked and pressed down flat on a sheet of paper.

A very rudimentary experiment in print-making can be made by drawing a simple image, such as a star, on a gum eraser, then cutting away (to the depth of about an eighth of an inch) the surface outside the area of the star. The eraser is then used like a stamp. When the raised part (the star) is covered lightly with ink, then pressed firmly onto a sheet of paper, the required image will remain on the paper when the eraser is removed. This is the simplest kind of print that can be made. The most complicated kind is typified by the engraving opposite. Every detail of the drawing was tooled by hand on a steel plate from which the subject could be printed in quantity. And what a long, painstaking job this must have been.

Before the advent of photography, prints were often made to document history, and how interesting they are for this reason, as well as for the great detail and preciseness of the artist's linework. This print shows the great sixteenth-century queen at the height of her power following England's defeat of the supposedly invincible Spanish fleet. And how proud she looks. ("Queen Elizabeth I." After a drawing by C. de Passe. Engraved by C. Turner. Pierpont Morgan Library.)

On this steel engraving, made from a drawing by Callot, we see the Spanish Army being organized for battle shortly before the defeat of the Dutch in 1625. ("Siege of Breda." Jacques Callot. Museum of Fine Arts, Boston.)

96

Israel siluestre ex Parisijs.   Cum priuil. Regis.   Iac. Callo. Le fec.

Even before Beatrix Potter's day, artists envisioned mice as human beings, as we learn from this woodcut of four scholars in Japan. After a drawing is traced onto a block of wood, it takes a steady hand to chip the surface away so that the lines, especially the thin, curving ones, remain unbroken, and will print as crisply as they do in this delightful example. ("Mice." Katsushika Hokusai.)

Woodcuts, lithographs, and etchings are called "original prints" because not only is the subject drawn directly on the printing surface, but the prints are pulled on a hand-operated press in a limited quantity. The number of copies issued might be as few as fifty or a hundred. The larger the edition—and it may go into hundreds—the less expensive the print is likely to be. Sometimes the size of the edition depends upon the intricacy of the drawing; those in several colors, for instance, require a separate block and a separate impression for each color.

Anyone who has tried to draw a horse rolling knows what skill it takes—particularly to do it as well as this Japanese master demonstrates. ("Horses" [Woodcut].) Katsukawa Shunsho.)

Overleaf: The butterflies on the next pages, from an old Japanese book, were printed in green, purple, and yellow. This meant that a separate woodblock had to be made to print each color. (Kamisaka. From his *A Thousand Butterflies.* Yamada Seiso.)

1 *Perennial dwarf Sun flower*	8 *Pansies, or Hearts-ease.*	17 *Fraxinella.*	26 *White Jasmine.*
Ultamarine & Prusian blen	9 *Maidens blush Rose.*	18 *Moss province Rose.*	27 *Scarlet Geranium.*
2 *Iris Major.*	10 *Yellow Jasmine.*	19 *Double Tirginian Silk-grass.*	28 *Yellow Martagon.*
3 *Blew Nigella.*	11 *Blew Corn flower.*	20 *White Rose.*	29 *Red Martagon.*
or Fennel flower.	12 *Blush Belgick Rose.*	21 *Dutch Hundred Leav'd Rose.*	30 *Teucrium or Germander.*
4 *Moon Trefoile.*	13 *The Francford Rose.*	22 *White Batchelors Button.*	31 *Mountain dwarf Pink.*
5 *Upright Sweet William.*	14 *Double Martagon.*	23 *Rosa Mundi.*	32 *Yellow Corn Mary gold.*
6 *Saxifrage.*	15 *Orchis or Bee flower.*	24 *Mountain Lychnis.*	33 *Purple sweet Pea.*
7 *Cinque foile.*	16 *Scarlet Colutea.*	25 *Dwarf Iris Strip'd.*	34 *Greek Valerian.*

JUNE

Delin et sculp ? *sketch*

From the Collection of Rob.? Furber, Gardner at Kensington. 1730?

Engrav'd by H.? Fletcher.

The nineteenth-century print-makers Currier and Ives employed artists to draw subjects they knew the American public would like. They then made colored prints from the originals and sold them by the thousands. ("U.S. Frigate *Constitution*." Currier and Ives.)

Opposite: People who love flowers will appreciate every detail of this fine eighteenth-century engraving of English horticultural specimens. ("June." Engraving by H. Fletcher. The Old Print Shop, New York.)

Nearly always, it is possible to distinguish a limited-edition print from a reproduction, if in no other way than by the two figures an artist places directly under the picture. These indicate the total quantity of the edition, and also the specific number of the print you are looking at, which will have been marked according to the order in which it was lifted from the press.

Other prints, however, such as the engravings on these pages, may have been run in an edition of thousands. When so many prints are made, there is no particular value in numbering each copy.

No artist has equaled Audubon for the quality and quantity of his bird studies. He made 435 compositions for the original set of prints which were engraved, printed, and hand-colored in London during the years 1827–1838. Audubon brought the touch of a poet to his work as an ornithologist. It is this element as well as his classic training in the studio of the French painter David that contributed to his greatness. (*Left:* "Saw-Whet Owl." *Opposite:* "Red-shouldered Hawks." John James Audubon.)

Opposite: The artist relied on deft lines to give dimension and human character to this highly stylized etching. This technique of print-making calls for the drawing to be traced, then etched into a copper plate from which the picture is printed. ("Old Man Figuring." Paul Klee. Museum of Modern Art.)

Above: This lithograph by Rouault relies on light and shadow for its powerful effect. Lithographs are made by drawing on a special stone surface with a wax crayon. The surface is then covered with acid which eats it away around the resisting crayon lines. When inked, these lines will print on paper pressed flat against the stone. ("Self-portrait with Cap." Georges Rouault. Museum of Modern Art.)

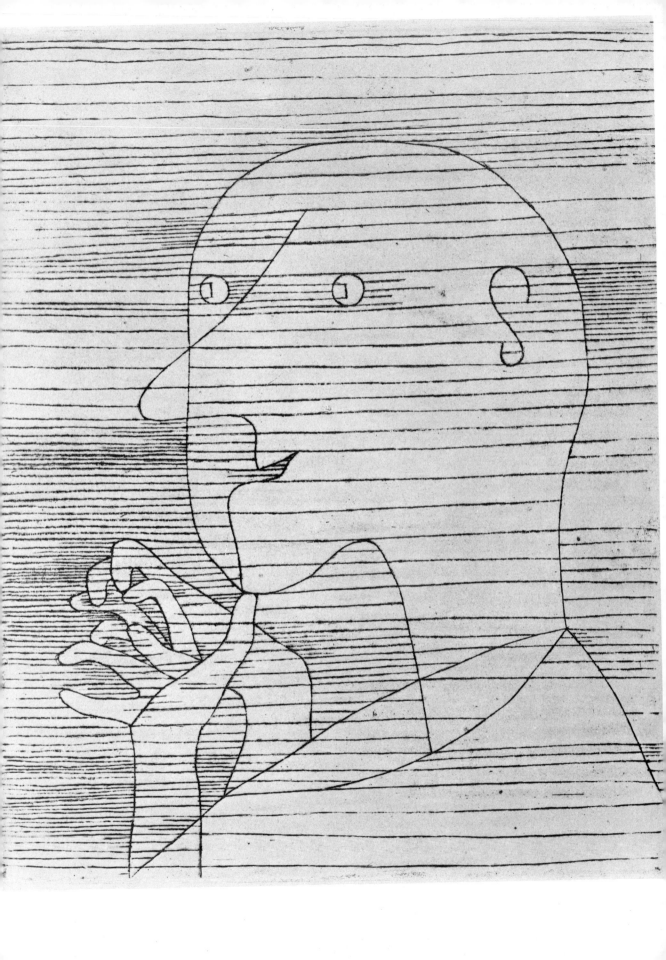

The Open Book

A quite different kind of drawing is done by the artist who illustrates a story. In early days such drawings were meticulously executed in ink, gold, and water color, directly on the parchment of a hand-lettered manuscript. Because everything was done by hand, only one copy of a book could be produced, and this priceless treasure was usually designed for some very special person or occasion. *The Book of Tournaments of King René I of Anjou,* from which the illustration overleaf has been taken, is a splendid example of the so-called illuminated manuscript. Most of the existing medieval examples, however, are Latin Bibles, copied out by hand and illuminated by monks in their monasteries.

After the invention of the printing press in the fifteenth century, it became possible to print black-and-white drawings in much the same way that they are reproduced in books today. An example from the seventeenth century is the eager-looking knight on the left-hand page.

Artists are usually called upon to illustrate books that other people have written. While it does occur that an artist is also a good writer, or that a writer is able to illustrate his own books, the combination of the two talents is rare. Rarer still is the person who excels in both media. This was just as true in the old days as it is now.

Opposite: In the days "when knights were bold," they encased themselves in steel for the lists as well as for the more serious business of war itself. The armor was sometimes so heavy that a crane had to be employed to hoist the knight onto the horse's back. And there he was likely to stay until an opponent knocked him off. ("Knight on Horseback." Unknown seventeenth-century French artist.)

Overleaf: The watercolor on the next two pages is from a rare fifteenth-century illuminated manuscript in which every moment of a royal medieval tournament is superbly presented. The scene shows the Duke of Brittany entering the town with his attendants. (From *The Book of Tournaments of King René I of Anjou.*)

Here is the Spaniard in the classic novel by Cervantes, who fancied himself a knight and whose acts of chivalry were always landing him in difficulties. ("Don Quixote with Sancho Panza." Honoré Daumier. Knoedler Galleries.)

Not all interpretations of stories have been done expressly for a book or magazine. For instance, Daumier illustrated *Don Quixote* (above) simply because he found the legendary Spaniard whose mind played such games with him an intriguing subject to draw. Other artists have done the same, and for much the same reason Delacroix made his own interpretations of *Hamlet,* one of which appears on the facing page.

When a well known novel or play is to be reprinted, a publisher will very often ask an artist to illustrate a special edition. This can present a much greater challenge to the artist than making a set of drawings for an entirely new story, for here he has to try to please readers who already know the book or play in question and have very definite ideas of their own about how each character looks and dresses. Indeed, when one of the great artists of our day, Salvador Dali, illustrated a limited edition

Opposite: "That skull had a tongue in it, and could sing once: how the knave jowls it to the ground, as if it were Cain's jaw-bone, that did the first murder!" (The gravediggers' scene in Shakespeare's *Hamlet.* Eugène Delacroix. Albertina Museum, Vienna.)

of *Macbeth,* no one had ever thought of Macbeth in quite the way that Dali drew him. However, this edition of Shakespeare's play, from which the illustration below is taken, is highly prized by collectors.

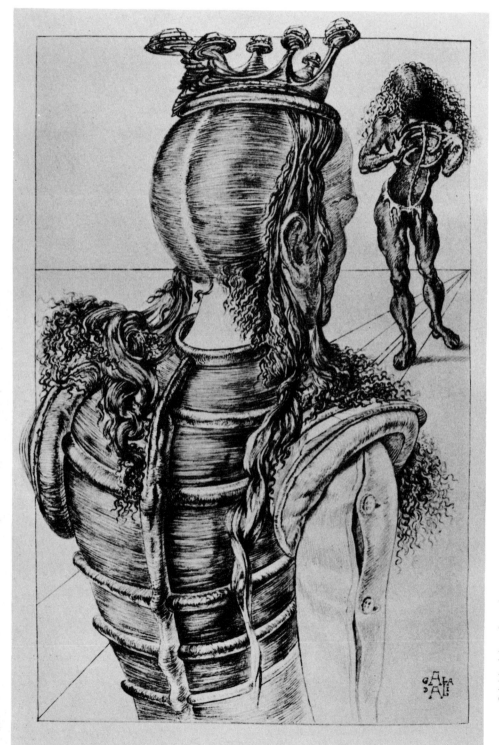

Left: A highly original interpretation of a scene from *Macbeth,* designed for a 1946 edition of Shakespeare's tragedy. (Illustration by Salvador Dali for *Macbeth.* Doubleday.)

Opposite: In the spirit of one of Poe's poems is this moonlit, bat-haunted view of Rome's Coliseum, also drawn by a present-day artist. (Lithograph by Hugo Steiner-Prag for *The Poems of Edgar Allan Poe.* Limited Editions Club, © 1943.)

The execution of Lady Jane Grey. A gruesome scene, described with equal vividness in the famous novel based on the life of the tragic young lady who was queen for nine days. (Illustration by George Cruikshank for *The Tower of London* by William Harrison Ainsworth. Richard Bentley.)

"Look at that monster with the pointed tail who passes mountain walls and shatters weapons." (Illustration by Gustave Doré for *The Divine Comedy* by Dante.)

Left: The little girl as she first appeared in a scene from Carroll's classic and as she has continued to appear in every edition since. (Illustration by John Tenniel for *Alice in Wonderland* by Lewis Carroll.)

Above: Miss Potter's story-book animals are typified in this cozy bedtime scene drawn in 1893, eight years before her first book, *The Tale of Peter Rabbit,* was privately published. (Sketch from *The Art of Beatrix Potter.* Frederick Warne and Co.)

Within the last hundred years, most book illustrations have been made for children's stories. Perhaps the best known is *Alice in Wonderland,* which Lewis Carroll wrote and John Tenniel illustrated to the delight, as it turned out, of readers of all ages. Although the story is all-important, one cannot possibly imagine the book without the illustrations. To everyone who has read this classic—and can there be anyone who has not enjoyed *Through the Looking Glass* too?—Alice *is* a Tenniel drawing. Had neither of the stories been illustrated in the first place, everyone's idea of the little girl with the long hair, the White Rabbit, the Mad Hatter, the Cheshire Cat, and all the other fanciful characters would be quite different.

The same can be said of the *Tale of Peter Rabbit,* which Beatrix Potter wrote and illustrated with such charm. It is hard to believe that when Miss Potter set out to show her little bundle of enchantment to publishers in London it was a very long time before she found any one of these worthy gentlemen in the least bit interested in the affairs of Mr. McGregor's garden. But never in all these years has the book been out of print. The same is true of all her other stories.

Today the same kind of enchantment goes on. After reviewing the distasteful subject of cats with Bernard, Miss Bianca's "lovely eyes were for a moment veiled. Then one small pink hand crept up to finger the silver chain." (Illustration by Garth Williams for *The Rescuers* by Margery Sharp. Little, Brown.)

Above: Tom found him "laying there, sound asleep on the floor." A famous scene from a very famous book. (Illustration made in two colors by Thomas H. Benton for *The Adventures of Tom Sawyer* by Mark Twain. Limited Editions Club, © 1939.)

Opposite: With her mind filled with romantic thoughts of Heathcliff, Cathy looks across the lonely, windswept moors of Yorkshire, wishing he were there. (Proposed illustration by Balthus for *Wuthering Heights* by Emily Brontë. Pierre Matisse Gallery.)

Left: A tender moment from another of the world's great love stories. (Illustration by Josep Nicolas for *The Romance of Tristan and Iseult,* retold by Joseph Bédier. Pantheon Books.)

Opposite: "Their ship sailed upon the waters of the Great Sea. Its carved prow cut the waves like a sharp plow." A decorative page from the Russian folk tale of seven brothers in the days of the great King Douda. (Illustration by Boris Artzybasheff for his *Seven Simeons*. Viking.)

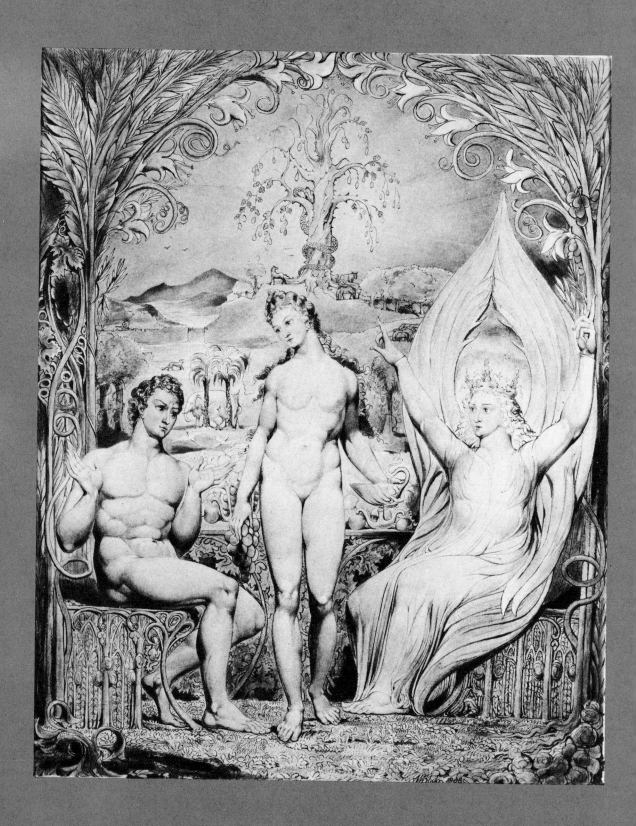

The Muses

While some artists are content to represent the outward appearances of people and the world about them, others enjoy giving full rein to their imagination. Religion, poetry, music, and drama inspire them, and occasionally they try their hand at astrological subjects as did the Persian artist who drew the Gemini twins on page 136. But probably nothing is more likely to make the romantically inclined artist reach for pencil and paper than a memory of some weird or wonderful dream.

Hieronymus Bosch of fifteenth-century Holland was a painter of the weird, and the visions of William Blake, the eighteenth-century English mystic, included Adam and Eve as interpreted on the opposite page. Nearer to our times is Redon, and in our very own day artists such as Dali, Tchelitchew, and Berman have continued to bring poetry to life in marvelously graphic ways.

One could easily imagine that a clear starry night gave birth to the first romantic drawing. Or perhaps it evolved from an impression on one of those windy days when the clouds form and reform themselves into all sorts of abstract and semi-human shapes. Had the changing outline of a cloud suddenly declared itself to the artist's eye as a lady with a harp, or shaped itself into a horse or a dragon as impossibly wild as the one over the page, little more would have been required of his imagination to start constructing a whole series of scenes around this fabulous pageant of the skies, just as the Greeks did in their ancient writings.

"For man to tell how human life began is hard; for who himself beginning knew?" In a scene from Milton's *Paradise Lost,* Adam discourses with Raphael in the Garden of Eden. Behind the standing figure of Eve, Satan, in the form of a serpent, entwines the "Tree of Life," from which he later tempts her to pick the forbidden fruit. ("Raphael with Adam and Eve." William Blake. Museum of Fine Arts, Boston.)

Poets and dreamers often gaze at the sky, enjoying the ever changing patterns of clouds as they pass, and who knows but that the shape of some particularly weird and beastlike formation first suggested the idea of a dragon? ("Mythological Beast." [Detail]. Unknown seventeenth-century Chinese artist. Metropolitan Museum of Art.)

Opposite: A vase decoration inspired by a mythological poet named Mousaios. The detail shows Aphrodite and the Muses. (A Greek vase. Meidias artist. Metropolitan Museum of Art.)

A modern interpretation of the combat of Perseus and Phineus over Andromeda. (Etching by Pablo Picasso for Ovid's *Metamorphoses*. Albert Skira.)

Opposite: Few drawings or paintings sum up the words *poetry* and *music* so sensitively as this study in pastel. According to Greek legend, after Orpheus was slain, his head floated down the Hebrus and came ashore at Lesbos, where a shrine was built in his name. ("Orpheus." Odilon Redon. The Cleveland Museum of Art.)

At times the weather, as well as environment, strongly influences the way we feel. On a rainy day some people find it easier to say No to everything, and on a bright sunny day to say Yes. And dreary days, if one allows them to, can evoke a nostalgic mood or the sort of brooding and sadness Emily Brontë experienced on those cold and lonely Yorkshire moors she wrote about in *Wuthering Heights* and which illustrators have since tried their hand at interpreting, as seen earlier on page 121.

But it is the stormy night that is likely to inspire the wildest kinds of imaginings. The sight of a dark ghoulish sky and the sound of wind howling or moaning through the treetops might provide the moment to draw one of those haunted landscapes

A combination of an artist's dreams, imagination, and technical skill produced this triumphal procession. The carcass of some fearful, dragon-like beast is transported through

filled with tortured souls, devils, and demons such as Gustave Doré imagined while he was illustrating Dante's *Divine Comedy*. And at the height of a thunderstorm how easy it is to visualize a scene like the one in *Macbeth* when the ghost of the king materializes from a fork of lightning and descends across the turrets of Dunsinane to face his murderer.

Artists and writers, equally, have taken a hand in adding fancy to fact. Grimm's fairy tales (somehow so aptly named) and the stories of Hans Andersen, many of them, are dreams. And so was Shakespeare's vision of a midsummer night, which he masterfully wove into a play.

a dark swampland—to the understandable alarm of the ducks at left. ("The Carcass" [Print]. Agostino de' Musi. Rosewald Collection, National Gallery of Art, Washington.)

Man's ever growing interest in life on other planets is reflected in a world of craters wherein gravity—or the lack of it—allows everything to stand, or hang, as conveniently upside down as upside up. ("Another World." Maurits Escher. Rosewald Collection, National Gallery of Art, Washington.)

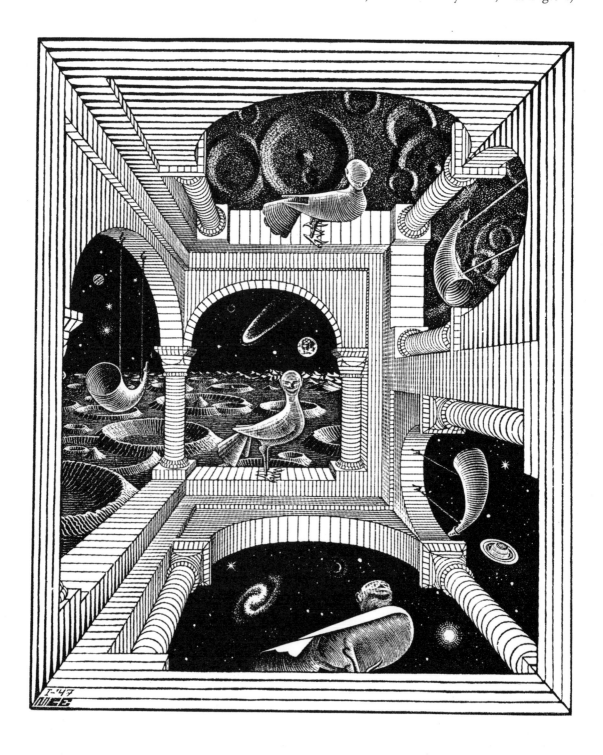

Some say that an owl circling overhead is an omen of bad luck; some say just the opposite. But on a stormy night, who wouldn't be scared if this one screeched past, suddenly, in the dark? (Drawing by Richard Lindner for *The Tales of Hoffman.* Wyn.)

Left: Even portraits can
endowed with a star-studd⸻
other-world quality. ("Z⸻
rina." Pavel Tchelitche⸻
Museum of Modern Art.)

Opposite: And here mu⸻
itself is represented in
ethereal human form. ("M⸻
sic." Eugene Berman. Juli⸻
Levy Gallery.)

In yet another medium, composers have written symphonies and tone poems which, if not interpretive of emotions or dreams or fantasies, can certainly evoke them. Like the weather, music sometimes influences an artist's choice of a subject, and even the way he guides his pencil or brush in the execution of it, as opposite. Perhaps this is because the elements which he wishes to combine in his work stem from that same "somewhere" that his favorite composer discovered deep down in himself. In any event, one can imagine that a drawing produced to the accompaniment of a thundering Beethoven symphony would be very different from one inspired, for instance, by the music of Respighi or Ravel.

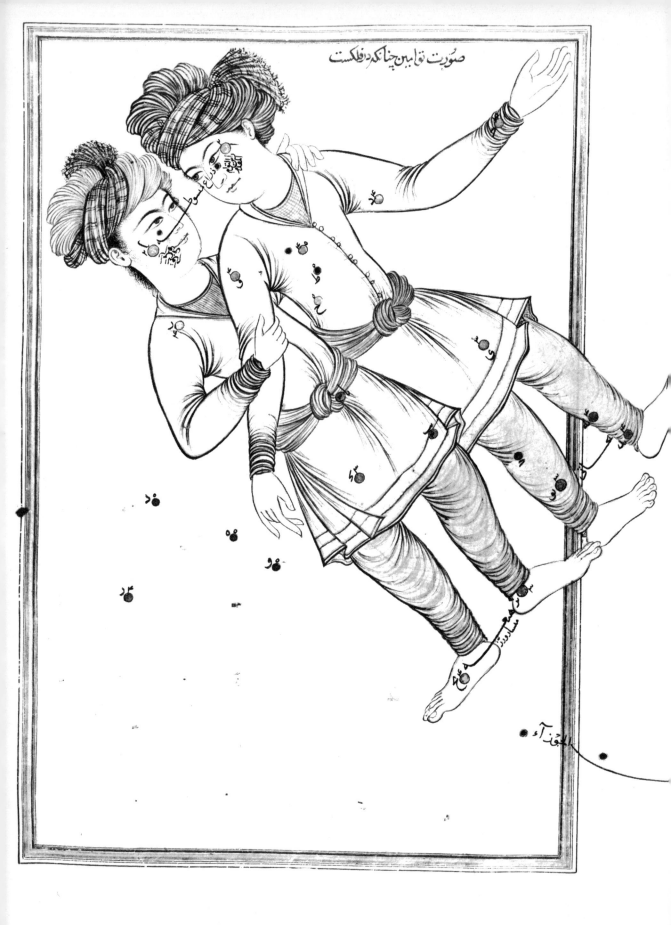

Opposite: According to the book, those born between May 21 and June 21 have a dual personality—as well balanced, it is to be hoped, as these twins riding on stars. ("Gemini Twins." From *The Book of Stars and Constellations.*)

Where else but in a fairy tale would one expect to see such a fantastic illustration? Yet, in fact, this was a real warrior, drawn in the eighteenth century by the same hand that created the comedy of mice on page 98. With a change of mask, good artists, like good actors, bring very different characters to life. ("Chinese Warrior." Katsushika Hokusai.)

When several people get together and make a drawing such as the one above, it might turn out to be rather like a game of Heads, Bodies, and Legs, in which a drawing is passed from hand to hand and added to with increasingly fanciful results. ("Cadavre Exquis." Composite drawing by André Breton, Tristan Tzara, Valentine Hugo, and Greta Knutson. Museum of Modern Art.)

Opposite: This fish-headed creature is a Singhalese demon named Rahu Asurilu who, according to Hindu legend, has the power to cause the eclipse of the sun and moon. (Illustration from an eighteenth-century Indian manuscript. Bibliothèque Nationale, Paris.)

A Time to Laugh

The best humorous drawings surely belong to our own century. We feel this not just because some of the things that amuse us today are different from those that our fore-fathers considered funny, but because modern cartoonists put their jokes across with fewer words—sometimes with no words at all—and with a simpler kind of drawing. In any century and in any country economy of line in drawing is a virtue, and the ancient Chinese and Japanese artists were the first to say so and prove it. A few well chosen lines can be as effective or funny as a few well chosen words.

Today we are as free and easy with our wit as we appear to be in the fit of our clothes. That things used to be very different is evident from the drawing on page 143. The lady whose skirt makes such a commodious umbrella for the pullets is so pinched in at the waist that she could hardly have risked a laugh even if she had felt like giving in to one. In her day, we have been told, it was more genteel to giggle than to laugh, and more proper still not to giggle at all. But smiling apparently was all right, even in the best of Victorian circles, and perhaps that is the reason why most drawings of the last century produce in us little more than just that—a smile.

On the other hand it is hard to deny that the wild-looking ballet dancer opposite is both ludicrous and funny. Not everyone will think him equally amusing, for each of us has his own particular brand of humor, just as he has special preferences in clowns— and in all matters where taste is concerned.

It is hard to establish a definite dividing line between one kind of humorous draw-ing and another. At times, the distance is very short between a caricature and a cartoon, and between a cartoon and a drawing that is just plain funny. While the aim of a

When an ugly little man leaps on stage in an incongruously graceful pose, the caricature causes us to laugh, inwardly at least. ("Vestris Dancing." Unknown artist. Opera Museum, Paris.)

caricaturist is to extract the chief features of his subject, usually of his face, and exaggerate them as Hirschfeld has done with the characters in *My Fair Lady* on page 145, a cartoonist may do much the same while commenting on some current event. David Low's cartoon of Prime Minister Churchill and President Roosevelt at a crucial moment in World War II (on page 146) is both a caricature of the two great leaders and a satirical comment on political policy. Drawings of this nature are not necessarily as funny as they are witty.

Quite different is the drawing Constantin Alajálov made backstage at the opera, on page 149, and the one Peter Arno created of that now very famous man in the shower, on page 150. Both are the delightful kind of commentary on life that needs no word of explanation. It is abundantly clear in each instance just exactly what is going on.

The wonderfully ridiculous drawing by Tomi Ungerer on the last page of the book is equally eloquent. In the past an artist would probably have tried to explain such nonsense with a word or two, and what a pity this would have been.

Above: If a lady chooses to wear a skirt as wide as a tepee, why shouldn't three pullets enjoy nipping in and out of the shade? ("Pullets." Honoré Daumier. Philadelphia Museum of Art.)

Opposite: In political cartoons our sympathy is sometimes for the donkey—or for the man riding one and losing out to his rival. Undoubtedly the lady accompanying them on Wimbledon Common represents the voting public which both of these contestants are attempting to win. (Political cartoon. Thomas Rowlandson. British Museum.)

Right: A sketch that is partly straight portraiture and partly caricature. The lines only slightly exaggerate the way the artist looked when he drew himself. Most self-portraits are kinder than this one, which shows how candid Lautrec could be. ("Self-portrait." Henri de Toulouse-Lautrec. From *Lautrec by Lautrec.* Edita.)

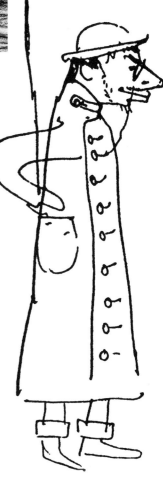

An amusing way of out-
lining an unamusing little
man. At once he becomes
the focus of our sympa-
thetic attention. (Cartoon.
Fougasse.Courtesy,*Punch.*)

Not only a great caricature, but a wonderful drawing of the principal actors in the historic musical based on Bernard Shaw's *Pygmalion*. (Stanley Holloway, Julie Andrews, and Rex Harrison in *My Fair Lady*. Al Hirschfeld. Courtesy, *The New York Times*.)

A timely World War II political cartoon that asked what the real dividing line was between aiding free Europe and defending the United States. This graphic comment was prompted by the signing of the Lend Lease bill by Roosevelt and Churchill. ("Lend Lease." David Low. Courtesy, *The Evening Standard.*)

In his cartoons Disney is usually caricaturing people more than he is the animals—and birds—that animate the story. Thus we are apt to laugh harder when we recognize ourselves mixed up in Donald than we do at the mixed-up duck himself. (Donald Duck. © Walt Disney Productions.)

Opposite: Even without the Eiffel Tower, where else could the gay scene be but in Paris? This was the day that the Spanish ambassador moved in next door with a son in a horrible hat. (Illustration by Ludwig Bemelmans for his *Madeline and the Bad Hat.* Viking.)

146

Above: The cartoons of Thurber center on the theme of the hen-pecked husband and the domineering wife—whose image often appeared to him much larger than life. ("Home." James Thurber. Copyr. © 1935, James Thurber. Copyr. © 1963 Helen W. Thurber and Rosemary Thurber Sauers. Originally published in *The New Yorker.*)

Opposite: Opera magic, so much of it, depends upon a stagehand who is well trained and, as suggested here, well *meaning* too. A tense moment with the wires in *Lohengrin.* (Drawing. Alajálov. Copr. © 1937, 1965. *The New Yorker Magazine, Inc.*)

But of course the train cannot follow both tracks at once. No cartoonist but Addams could be so entertainingly macabre. ("Suicide Pact." Charles Addams. Copr. © 1945. *The New Yorker Magazine, Inc.*)

Opposite: When an amusing thought is superbly drawn, a cartoon remains great forever. (Man in the shower. Peter Arno. Copr. © 1943. *The New Yorker Magazine, Inc.*)

"Here we are at St. Custards, poised between past and future." Many schoolboys have felt like doing this, but how often have they had the courage—or the ready cash for the powder? (Illustration by Ronald Searle for *Molesworth,* with text by Geoffrey Williams. Max Parrish.)

The things some dogs have to put up with! ("**** you, you, ****-****!" by Ronald Searle from *The Dog's Ear Book,* with text by Geoffrey Williams. Max Parrish.)

Below: A caricature not only of a dachshund but of a dog who knows he shouldn't have stolen it but is absolutely delighted that he did. ("Hansi." Ludwig Bemelmans.)

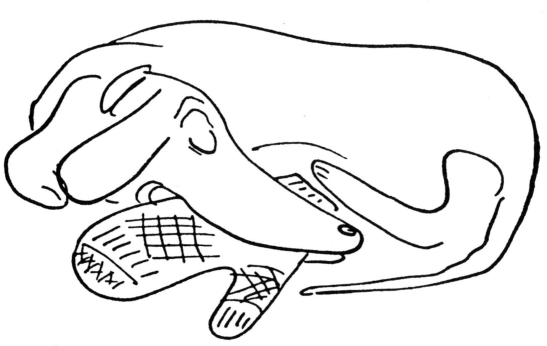

Most cartoons—and all those by Steinberg—carry no written legend. So it is up to us to interpret, or merely to be entertained by, this drawing of a determined little man leaping from a pinnacle to a post fit for a Caesar. (Drawing. Saul Steinberg. Copr. © 1961. *The New Yorker Magazine, Inc.*)

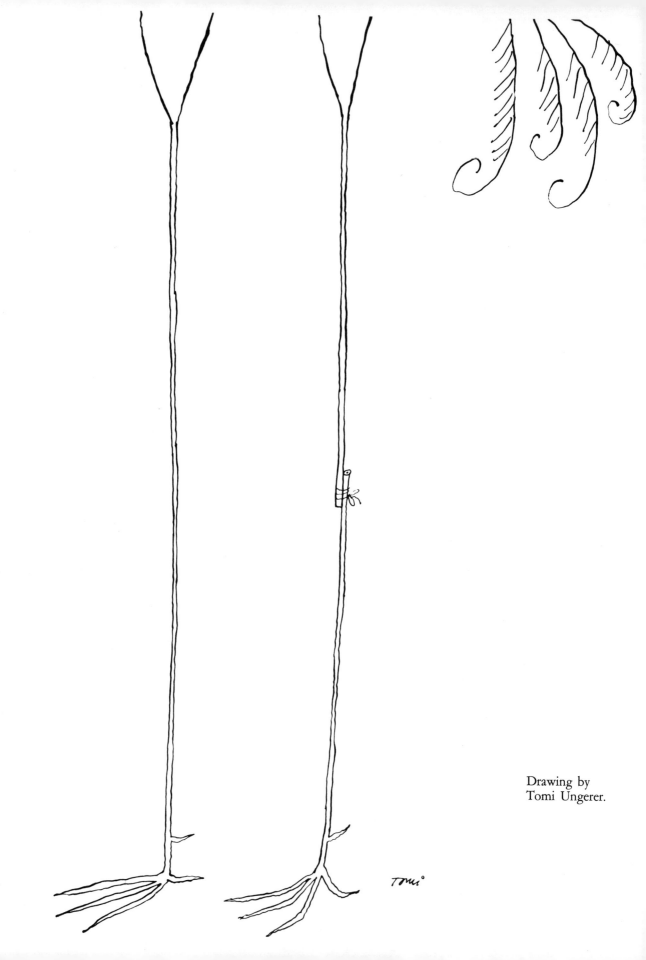

Drawing by
Tomi Ungerer.

Index of Artists

(folios in italics indicate illustration)

About the Author

For more than thirty years Bryan Holme has been an editor and publisher of art books in New York, following in the footsteps of his father, Charles Geoffrey Holme, and his grandfather, Charles Holme, who was the founder of *Studio,* a magazine of major importance in the international world of art at the turn of the century.

Bryan Holme has carried on the tradition of Studio books, and the Studio imprint appears on some thirty volumes a year published in the United States under his guidance. He has written several books of his own and has been co-author and designer of many more on various aspects of art, photography, travel, architecture, and decoration.

His hobbies might be called "busman's hobbies," for he enjoys taking photographs (many have appeared in books, magazines, and newspapers), he paints, loves to travel; he collects art and is obsessed with old houses, which, with his family, he enjoys restoring and decorating.

Raoul Dufy